JULIAN'S DRAGONS

Jodie Graham
Illustrations by Marcy Petricig Braasch

Julian's Dragons

iUniverse books may be ordered through booksellers or by contacting:

iUniverse
1663 Liberty Drive
Bloomington, IN 47403
www.iuniverse.com
1-800-Authors (1-800-288-4677)

ISBN: 978-1-5320-8821-6 (sc)
978-1-5320-8822-3 (e)

Library of Congress Control Number: 2019918207

Print information available on the last page.

iUniverse rev. date: 12/06/2019

Julian has dragons he locks up inside.

His dragons are fierce and don't like to hide.

Dragons help Julian keep
bad things away.

They're with him at home and
in school through the day.

The dragons stay on guard,
strong and alert.

They don't want Julian ever to
be hurt.

They will break loose when
they fear there is danger.

And without warning, his
chest tightens with anger.

His heart beats so fast, like a deep, pounding drum.

His body is on fire! His head becomes numb!

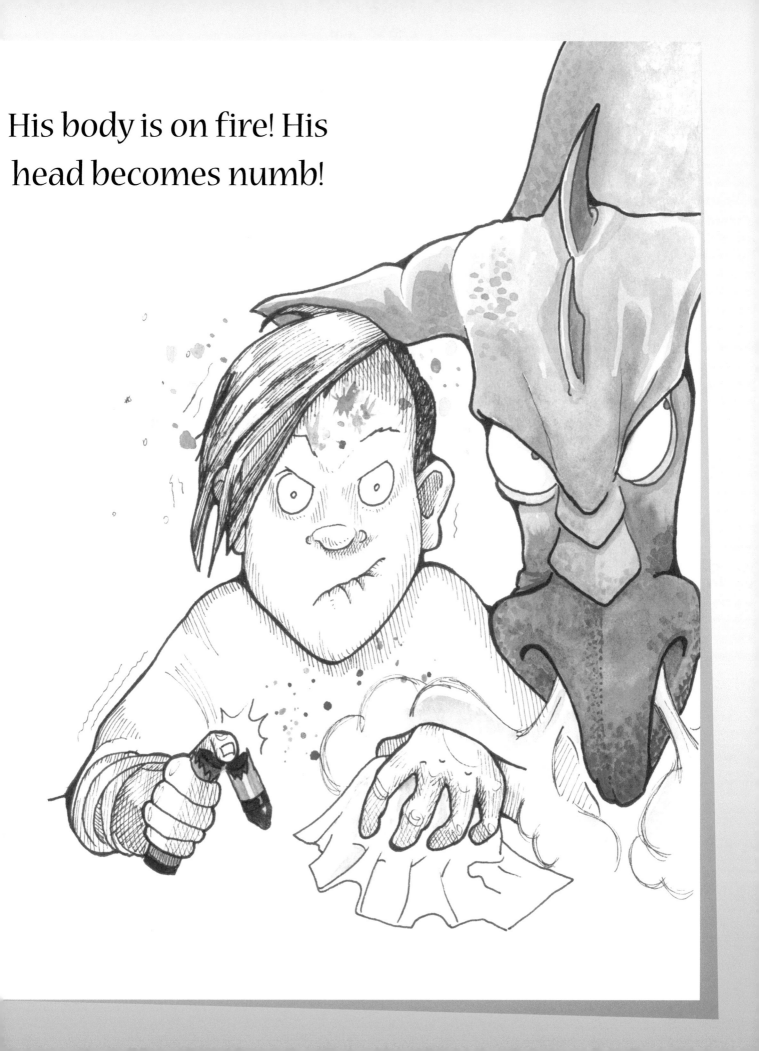

Dragons unleashed!

They are now out in the open.

Kicking and screaming is
how Julian is coping.

They fight!

And they rage until his
body is worn out!

Julian is now safe, the dragons do not doubt.

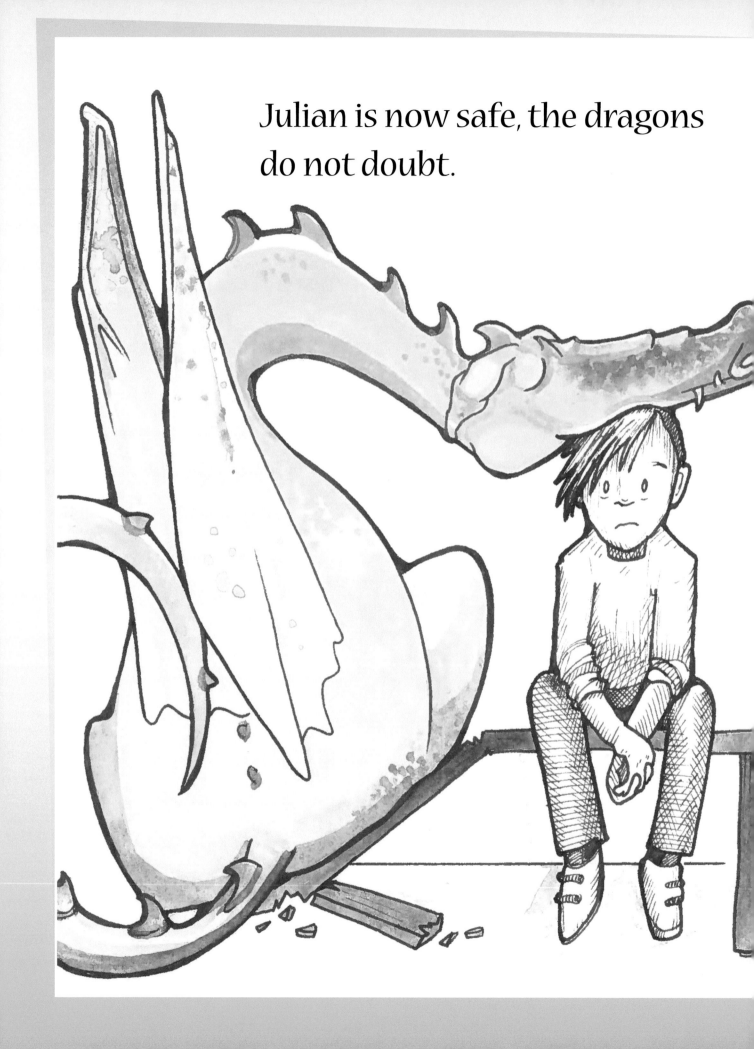

Dragons are his protectors.

They know Julian best.

He must be defended before they will rest.

The battle is over, and the dragons go back to hide.

Will they ever leave?

he wonders inside.

Dragons want to help out,

but they don't always know

when it's right to come out,

and when they should go.

All kids have dragons. He never knew!

So how does he control his?

What more can he do?

Julian tries to ignore them
to make them go away.

But the harder he tries, the
more they want to stay.

Julian does not want to feel.

He does not want to think.

But the dragons just get bigger,

and he

has started

to

shrink.

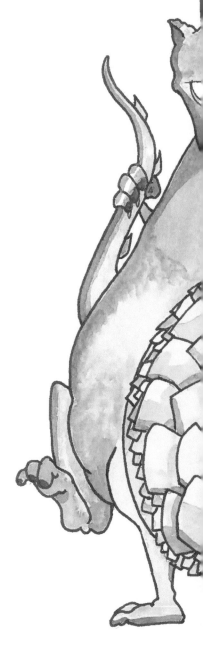

Julian loves these dragons.

He doesn't want to blame them.

And one day, Miss G teaches
him how to tame them.

"We need our dragons to keep us safe and sound.

But there is a time and place for them to be around.

We have secret skills we can put into play

To help us with things that happen in our day."

And so she says gently,

"Count to three.

Now take a deep breath in.

Blow all the mad fire out.

Now do it again."

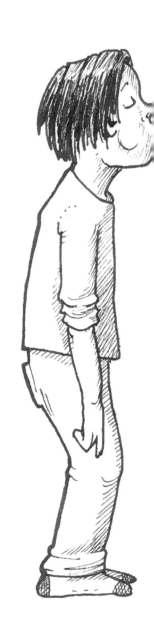

"Calm the loud drum that is
beating in your chest.

Tell those pesky dragons that
it is time for some rest."

"Squeeze your hands really tight, and then squeeze your toes.

Now release that deep breath out through your nose."

"As you breathe out,
go limp like spaghetti.

Wiggle every part until you
feel relaxed and ready."

"Gently close your eyes,

and let's calm your fear.

Tell me three things

that you

smell,

taste,

and hear."

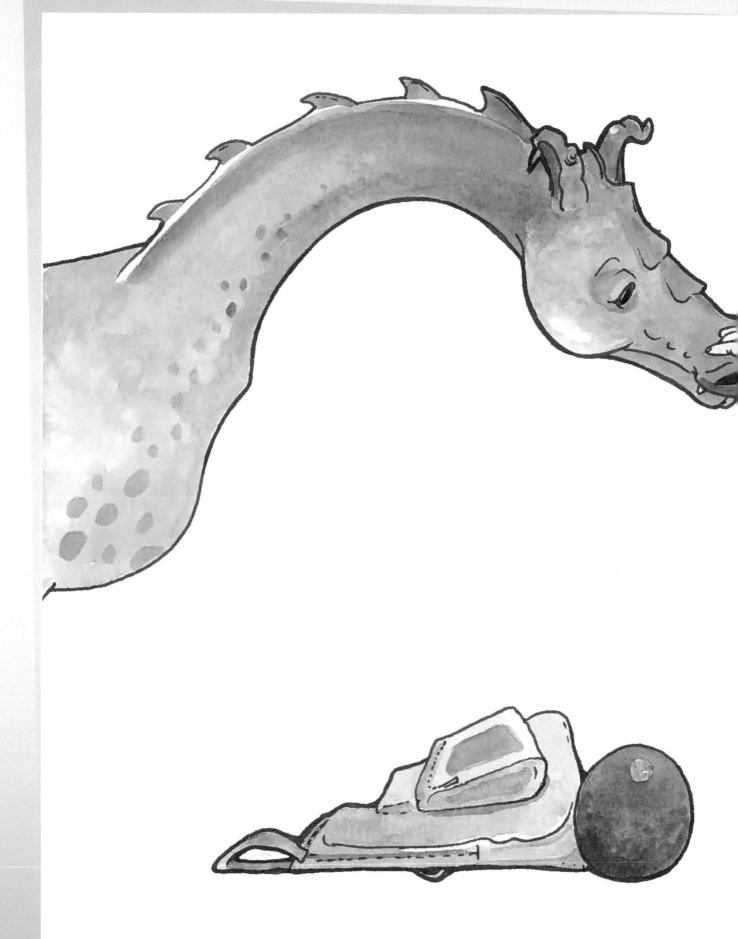

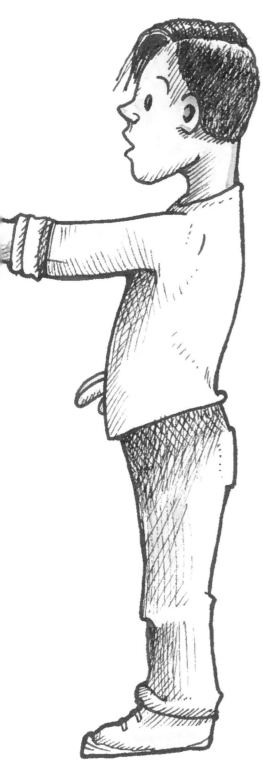

"Next time you feel the dragons
making your body tight,

Remember you have powers to
help them feel all right."

"The dragons help protect you.

They really mean you no harm.

But every now and then,

there will be a false alarm."

"So check in with your dragons
to make sure they're okay.

Check your body and your
breath to continue on with
your day."

Julian thanks Miss G with
a big smile on his face.

His dragons now live in
a happy, safe space.

Printed in the United States
By Bookmasters